PUFFIN BOOKS

UK | USA | Canada | Ireland | Australia | India | New Zealand | South Africa

Puffin Books is part of the Penguin Random House group of companies whose
addresses can be found at global.penguinrandomhouse.com.

www.penguin.co.uk
www.puffin.co.uk
www.ladybird.co.uk

Penguin
Random House
UK

First published 2016

001

Text and illustrations copyright © FremantleMedia Limited, 2016
Written by Kay Woodward
Illustrations by Lea Wade
The moral right of the author and illustrator has been asserted

Set in Sabon MT Std 15/23

Printed in Great Britain by Clays Ltd, St Ives plc

A CIP catalogue record for this book is available from the British Library

ISBN: 978–0–141–36682–1

All correspondence to
Puffin Books
Penguin Random House Children's
80 Strand, London WC2R 0RL

LICENCE TO CHILL

by Ernest Penfold

PUFFIN

The name's Penfold, Ernest Penfold.

I'm Danger Mouse's personal assistant and super sidekick and . . . drum roll . . . **BFF!**

What can I tell you about Danger Mouse? Well, firstly, he's the <u>greatest</u>. Secondly, he's <u>fantastic</u>. Thirdly, wherever there is **DANGER**, he'll be there. Which, fourthly, means that I'll be there too, because that's what sidekicks are for.

<u>**Gulp.**</u>

But the thing about super secret agents who think nothing of <u>parachuting into a volcano</u> or dangling off a cliff (before breakfast) is that they're usually too busy saving the world to write down how they do it. Though I can tell you that it's usually with some **BANGS** and **BOOMS** and an awful lot of **CRIKEYS** from me.

So let me introduce you to Danger Mouse's own personal reporter and biographer and storyteller . . . __ME!__ (Did you guess? You did? Oh.)

I'm great at multitasking — did you know that I can escape from an evil genius **AND** eat an ice cream at the same time? So I'm the ideal person to write about Danger Mouse's terrifyingly exciting adventures. When I'm not too scared to look, that is.

Over and out,

Penfold

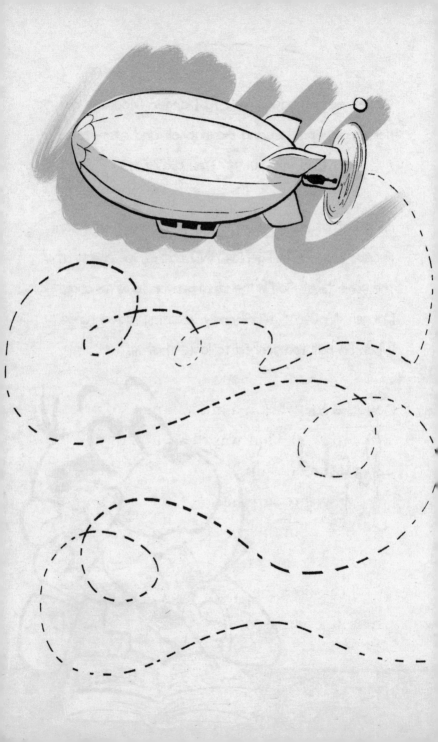

CHAPTER ONE

*B*rrrrrrrrr!
That wasn't me shivering. (Why would I shiver on a hot summer's day like today?) That was the sound of a miniature airship buzzing through the air like a bumblebee after a big dinner.

I tweaked the remote control to

send Professor Squawkencluck's latest invention left. It went left. I sent it right. Then I made the airship spin very, VERY slowly, like a tiny airborne ballerina.

Danger Mouse paused in the middle of a high-speed game of table tennis he was playing against himself. 'Steady on, Penfold,' he said. 'If you go any faster, the Red Arrows will be in touch to offer you a job.'

'Ha ha,' I said. 'Very funny, Chief.' (As well as being a super secret agent, my boss also thinks that he is a top comedian.)

'Um . . . Penfold?' whispered Danger Mouse out of the corner of his mouth.

'Yes, Chief?' I whispered back.

He winked. 'Is this one of *those* adventures? The ones where you write everything down and I get to star in a real-life book?'

I stopped scribbling and looked up from my notebook. 'Erm, yes. But don't do anything you wouldn't normally do,' I added hurriedly. 'Just ACT NATURAL.'

'No problem!' cried Danger Mouse. He flung the table-tennis bats aside, performed a neat swallow dive towards the airship's remote control and grabbed it. 'Now it's MY go!' he announced. 'I'll show you how it's done. Watch and learn, Penfold!'

'Noooooo!' I cried.

Last week, Danger Mouse had

accidentally destroyed a space periscope
when he'd used it to whack an asteroid
out of Earth's path. Professor
Squawkencluck had only just invented it.
Now she had officially banned him from
touching ANYTHING until the twenty-
second century, at least.

'Noooooooooooooooooooooooooooo
ooooooooooooooooooooooooooooooooo!'
I cried again, adding a few more Os this
time, just to make it REALLY clear.

Too late. Danger Mouse had the
remote control . . . and somehow I was
now riding the airship. (I'm not sure
how that happened, to be honest. It was
all a bit fast and I couldn't see for the
whooshes and flashes and whizzes and

pops. Look at the illustration. See what I mean?)

Now the airship was no longer
buzzing like a contented bee, but looping-
the-loop like a rocket-powered Spitfire –
and taking me with it.

'Wow!' I heard Danger Mouse say.
'Did you see what I did there? What skill!
What precision! Don't forget to put this
in the book. The readers will LOVE it.'

I was about to tell Danger Mouse that
readers might actually love to read about
me playing SAFELY with the airship,
but I bit my tongue. (Ouch.) I didn't
want Danger Mouse to think I was a
party pooper, so instead I made a note to
include his loop-the-loops, even though it
is NOT easy to make notes when you're
breaking the sound barrier.

Then I heard the one word guaranteed
to send terror into any sidekick's heart.

'Oops,' said Danger Mouse.

'What's wrong, Chief?' I gasped,
upside down now. Then the right way up.
Then back to front. I was starting to feel
a bit sick. Actually, a lot sick.

'You're not going to believe this,' he
replied. He stabbed all the buttons on the
airship's remote control and then shook it
like a snow globe. 'It's BROKEN.'

'DANGER MOUSE!' Squawkencluck
squawked from the broom cupboard,
where she was testing invisible ink.
'WHAT DID I TELL YOU?'

'Oops,' said Danger Mouse, again.

Which is when Colonel K's hologram

appeared in a burst of static. 'Attention!' boomed the Head of the British Secret Service. 'I have BAD NEWS!'

'Let me guess,' said Danger Mouse, rubbing his chin and staring thoughtfully into the middle distance. 'Baron Greenback has a brand-new, completely evil plan that's kicking off round about, um –' he checked his EyePatch – 'NOW?'

'By Jove,' said the Colonel. 'Not only are you the world's greatest super secret agent, but you're a mind reader too. Tell me more!'

Danger Mouse coughed politely. 'Oh, I couldn't possibly,' he said. 'No one likes a show-off.'

'Good show, old chum,' said the Colonel. 'Quite right. Now, before I reveal Baron Greenback's brand-new, completely evil plan, would someone please tell me what is causing that blasted *brrrrrrr*-ing?' He looked up. 'Oh, it's YOU, Penfilled. Better things to do, eh? Too busy to save the world like our hero down here, what?'

'S-s-s-sir –' I called from the ceiling of

HQ. (It's difficult not to stutter when the miniature airship you're riding is bouncing against the wall like a kangaroo that's had too many fizzy drinks.)

'I say,' said Colonel K, who'd already moved on, 'any chance of a drum roll around here? No? Shame. Anyway, I'm delighted to reveal that the weapon Baron Greenback will use to attempt to take over the world this week is . . .'

There was a long pause.

'Erm, Colonel?' said Danger Mouse. 'This is a fast-paced, action-packed book, starring me. Not a TV talent contest.'

'Ah, yes,' said the Colonel, blushing. 'Well, the Baron seems to have bought himself an enormous fridge-freezer.

It's almost certainly his brand-new, completely evil secret weapon.'

'Maybe he just wants to keep a large amount of food cool in a safe and hygienic way?' I suggested.

Danger Mouse raised an eyebrow. 'This is Baron Silas von Greenback we're talking about here, Penfold,' he said. 'His mission in life is to rule the world, not to banish bacteria.'

Meanwhile, I'd got the runaway airship completely under control again. I'd nearly reached the floor at the bottom of HQ. All I had to do was gently push away from the wall with my toes every three seconds and . . .

Oh, crikey. I flew straight out of the

letterbox into a day that suddenly didn't seem quite so summery and hot as it had ten minutes ago. It was positively chilly, in fact. I wished I'd worn a cardigan. And a vest.

But, even though I was suddenly freezing cold and just a little bit terrified of FLOATING AWAY AND BEING LOST FOREVER IN OUTER SPACE, I engaged my super-secret-agent's-sidekick powers and grabbed the edge of the letterbox as I sailed past. And I clung on.

'Don't worry, everyone! I can help Penfold!' Danger Mouse pointed to the sky, one hand on his chin, AND FROZE.

Oh, no. OH, NO. DISASTER! What could have happened? Had Danger

Mouse turned to stone? Had a dastardly villain poured freezing serum on to his cornflakes again? Or had our hero been immobilized by the ray of the (rare but totally deadly) ice-cream-and-jelly-fish?

Who would save the world NOW?

Who would save ME?

And, most importantly, how were we going to fill a book with action-packed adventure without Danger Mouse?!

'Heeeeeeeelp!' I sobbed.

'I told you, Penfold,' said Danger Mouse, still motionless. 'I'll save you!'

'You're ALIVE!' I cried.

'Of course I'm alive,' said Danger Mouse, unfreezing at last. 'I was just waiting for the illustrator to get a good action shot before I rescued you!'

Oh. Right. Great. It was a good job I wasn't in mortal danger.

'Excellent,' said Colonel. 'I'll leave you to it, then. Toodle-pip!' And he vanished in another *bzzzt* of static.

I peered nervously back in through the letterbox, my fingers slipping and my bones chilling. But Danger Mouse had already backflipped on to the emergency trampoline hidden behind the sofa and was rocketing upward, his rodent cheeks wibbling as if they belonged to a fighter pilot. Up, up and up he went, until he hit the ceiling with a DOINK, plummeted back down to the trampoline, bounced straight past me through the letterbox,

rebounded off a lamp post and finally
scooped me up and carried me back into
HQ. Squawkencluck's beloved airship
wasn't so lucky. It shot off in the direction
of Pall Mall.

Oops.

'Blimey, you weigh a ton, Penfold,'
puffed Danger Mouse, putting me down
on the floor of HQ with a loud clink.

Hang on. Just run that past me again.
A loud *clink*?

I, Ernest Penfold, sidekick to the
greatest super secret agent of them all,
did my best to open my mouth wider
than the Blackwall Tunnel and cry,
'HELP!' I would have done it too, if
I could have moved my mouth and my

tongue. But I couldn't, because (and here
we really did need that drum roll Colonel K
was after) I WAS FROZEN SOLID INSIDE
A BLOCK OF PENFOLD-SHAPED ICE.

CHAPTER TWO

*B*rrrrrrrrrr!
    (FYI, that *was* me shivering.)

Oh, crikey. Not only was I frozen as solid as an ice lolly, but the outside of HQ was frozen too. Icicles hung from the letterbox entrance like glittering teeth, imprisoning us inside.

I wiggled my eyes in despair.

'NOBODY PANIC!' shouted Danger Mouse. 'I am an expert linguist! I am fluent in a hundred and forty-three languages and I will instantly decode Penfold's eye movements to figure out exactly what he is saying.'

Phew. I would be defrosted in no time.

'*HELP*,' I blinked. '*I AM FROZEN INSIDE A BLOCK OF ICE. PLEASE RESCUE ME.*'

'Aha!' said Danger Mouse confidently. 'I think Penfold's trying to tell us that he's left the tap on.'

'*NO*,' I eyeball-wiggled. '*I ALWAYS TURN IT OFF. I AM IN DIRE, DEEP-FREEZE DANGER AND I NEED DEFROSTING. NOW.*'

'Ah, yes!' said Danger Mouse. 'Good old Penfold. He's reminding me that

I've got a dentist's appointment next week. Penfold, is it at two thirty? Get it, everyone? *Tooth hurty?* Ha ha!'

Hmm. Clearly Danger Mouse's language skills were not quite as good as his saving-the-world skills.

'Remember, remember the fifth of November . . . ?' tried the world's greatest secret agent. 'Red sky at night, shepherd's delight? Buy cheap, buy twice?'

I rolled my eyes.

'I've got it!' cried Danger Mouse. 'I think he wants us to DEFROST him!'

'Of course he does,' said Professor Squawkencluck, rolling her eyes too. 'Here, use this hairdryer.'

'Good thinking!' said Danger Mouse.

He grabbed the hairdryer, aimed and –

'No!' wailed Squawkencluck. 'Not
the too-cool-for-school button! I haven't
tested it yet!'

– FIRED AT ME.

A burst of blue flame shot out of
the hairdryer, totally surrounding me
in purple sparkles. (It was quite pretty,
actually.) The sparkles cleared and –
ta-daaaaaaa! – I was defrosted at last.

'It works!' cried Squawkencluck,
producing a hairdresser's mirror from up
her sleeve.

Whoa. My fringe was bigger than one
of the curtains at the Royal Opera House.

'What a hairstyle!' said Danger
Mouse. 'What a sidekick!'

But in the background something even more interesting than my cool new hairdo was happening. Squawkencluck's favourite TV programme – *The Geekly News* – had been zapped from the screens. The show was replaced by a zigzag pattern and a whole lot of hissing, and finally . . .

'MWAH HA HA!'

'Oh, goody,' said Danger Mouse, cracking his knuckles. 'I've been waiting for Greenback to pipe up. Friday afternoons are always so dull without an arch-villain.'

'IT IS I, BARON GREENBACK!' said Baron Greenback, grinning from the television screen.

'You don't say,' said Danger Mouse, lifting a super-cool eyebrow.

Stiletto, Greenback's right-hand crow, glared at Danger Mouse.

'I AM BROADCASTING MY EVIL MESSAGE TO EVERY TELEVISION IN THE WORLD, INCLUDING YOURS,

DANGER MOUSE. OH, YES I AM.'

'Is he going to speak in capital letters for the whole book, Chief?' I whispered. 'Only it takes up a lot more room and we'll have to stick some extra pages in the back if we want to squeeze in the whole adventure.'

'Good point, Penfold,' said Danger Mouse. He pressed his EyePatch. 'STOP SHOUTING,' he shouted. 'WE CAN HEAR YOU.'

'Erm . . . Mwah ha ha?' said Baron Greenback, more quietly. 'Is that better?'

'Much,' replied Danger Mouse. He deactivated the EyePatch and settled back to watch the screen.

'Excuse me, Chief,' I whispered to

Danger Mouse. 'If Baron Greenback is broadcasting his evil message to every television in the world, how can he be having a conversation with just you at the same time?'

Danger Mouse frowned. 'Good point, Penfold,' he said. 'I think you'll find that it's because of iambic frequencies and post-alveolar oscillation. Probably. Make sense? Excellent! Now, on with the show – oops! I mean, on with the BOOK!'

Baron Greenback's new secret lair seemed to be inside a giant lunchbox. (You could tell it was a lunchbox, because all the nice, chocolatey things had been eaten and there were just leftover giant carrot sticks and a huge salmon-spread

sandwich shrivelled in the corner.)

'Welcome to the new Ice Age!' Baron Greenback went on. 'I have a Fiendish Fridge-freezer and I'm not afraid to use it! Prepare to be cool for the first time ever!'

'I'm pretty cool already, thanks,' said Danger Mouse.

'Silence!' the Baron hissed. 'The freezing temperatures are just a warning! Unless your world leaders hand over *one squillion pounds* and complete control of Planet Earth, I shall turn the dial to deep-freeze on my FFF –'

'He means the Fiendish Fridge-freezer,' butted in Stiletto.

'Thanks, Stiletto,' said Danger Mouse. 'But it was only three paragraphs ago.

I think I can remember that FFF stands for Fiendish Fridge-freezer for that long.'

'Pfft,' huffed Stiletto, shaking his feathers.

'Excuse me?' said Baron Greenback. 'Are you all done now? I'd like to carry on taking over the world if that's OK?'

'Go for it,' said Danger Mouse. 'I'm here all week!' Then he muttered out of the side of his mouth, 'Actually, if we don't melt the icicle prison bars, Penfold, I will be here all week, which might make it a little bit tricky to save the world this afternoon –'

'Shush!' said Baron Greenback. He paused dramatically. 'And then the new Ice Age will begin!' he finished.

Everyone waited.

'*Barone?*' said Stiletto. 'Haven't you forgotten something?'

'Ah, yes,' added the Baron, baring his toady teeth. 'MWAH HA HA HA!'

CHAPTER THREE

'*In the bleak midwinter*
Frosty wind made moan,
Earth stood hard as iron,
Water like a stone –'

'Penfold?' said Danger Mouse.

'Yes, Chief?' I replied.

'Any chance you could stop singing Christmas carols? And maybe put the harp back in the cupboard?'

Chapter Three

'No problem!' I said, with festive cheer. 'Just getting into the swing of the wintry weather, Chief.'

Because outside HQ, it was *cold*. At least it looked cold, in a sparkly, icing-sugary way, beyond the industrial-strength icicles blocking the entrance and sealing us inside. But how could it be the bleak midwinter in August? And – oh! – did this mean that Christmas would come early too?! (Mmm . . . mince pies.)

'This means,' said Danger Mouse, thoughtfully stroking his chin, 'Baron Greenback must have kick-started his fiendish plan already. He froze Penfold, he's frozen HQ's exits shut so that we can't escape, and now he's begun to freeze the world with his FFF!' He paused and muttered under his breath, 'Erm, what does that stand for again?'

'Fiendish Fridge-freezer!' I said happily. I might not be any good at being fearless (or skydiving or operating a jet pack or finding that fiddly little plastic tag that opens a packet of biscuits with one easy tug), but remembering what abbreviations stand for? Easy.

Danger Mouse spun round. 'So what's going on with this FFF, Professor?'

'Well,' said Squawkencluck, snipping away at a roll of fluorescent fabric with a pair of crinkle-cut scissors. 'I think what the Baron's probably done is switched it on. That would account for all the ice.'

'Yes, absolutely,' said Danger Mouse, dropping to the floor and performing a few press-ups on one finger. 'Just getting limbered up here, Penfold. A super secret agent should never miss the chance to keep fit. Carry on, Professor.'

Squawkencluck put down her scissors and picked up some sticky-backed plastic. 'And I think that the reason this city isn't already a huge block of London-shaped ice is that the Baron hasn't turned the FFF's thermostat down yet. You know, to make it colder.'

'This calls for action stations!' cried Danger Mouse.

'Where are they on the tube map, Chief?' I said, whisking out my map of the London Underground. 'Are they on the Central line or the Jubilee?'

Squawkencluck looked up from her work, which now seemed to involve some sort of shiny-stamp collecting. 'Don't be silly, Penfold,' she said. 'They're not real

stations. It's just Danger Mouse's fancy
way of saying, "Ready, steady –"'

'GO!' I cried. I knew exactly what to
do. And while I was doing it I would show
Danger Mouse that I was the best sidekick
ever in the history of sidekicks. Even if I
did prefer doing things the safe way.

I blew on my palms to prepare myself.
I placed them carefully on the floor of
HQ and – avoiding the coffee table,
because the corners are very sharp –
performed a slow but perfect forward roll
in the direction of the kitchen. I sprang
elegantly to my feet. I reached for the jar
on the top shelf and made contact. Great!
Then, in one deft movement, I twisted off
the lid and plucked out . . . three teabags.

'Chief,' I said, giving him a slow nod. 'I'll put the kettle on now.'

'That's very thoughtful, Penfold,' said Danger Mouse. 'But I was sort of wondering if you might be able to do something a tiny bit more useful?'

I wasn't sure how ANYTHING could be more useful than a cup of tea – except perhaps two cups of tea and a plate of bourbon biscuits – but I put my plan B into operation immediately and grabbed a phone.

'Er, what are you doing now?' asked Danger Mouse.

'I'm ringing the world leaders to see who's got a spare one squillion pounds,' I said proudly. This was a plan B of champions. Danger Mouse would love it.

'Oh, no.' Danger Mouse shook his head firmly. 'First rule of outwitting master criminals: NEVER give in to ransom demands.'

'And I don't want to be picky,' said Squawkencluck, peering over her glasses at me, 'but technically there's no such thing as a squillion.'

Danger Mouse cleared his throat. 'I was sort of hoping that you might activate the computer's tracking system, find Baron Greenback and give me a precise GPS location so that we can shoot over there in the Danger Car and save the world by teatime.'

Oh, dear. As it happened, I wasn't

actually a hundred per cent sure how to
switch the computer on.

'*Ta-daaaaa!*' Squawkencluck held up
a pair of bright yellow wide-bottomed
trousers covered with glittering squares.
'Solar flares!' she announced.

Typical. Squawkencluck had managed
to invent a whole new fashion item, and
I hadn't done a thing.

'They're super insulated and
guaranteed to keep the wearer warm
in temperatures as low as -100°C!'
Squawkencluck said proudly. 'And the
way they work is completely brilliant.
All you need to do is –'

'Wear them!' finished Danger
Mouse, grabbing the solar flares from

Squawkencluck's hands.

Right. I had to prove to everyone what a brilliant sidekick I was. And five minutes later, I'd done it! I HAD SWITCHED THE COMPUTER ON.

In the meantime, though, Danger Mouse had already used his EyePatch to pinpoint the Baron's location to within three millimetres, *and* he'd tried on the solar flares and done a star jump in them and ripped the seams.

Squawkencluck whisked the flares away, muttering crossly to herself.

'Ohhh,' I wailed. 'I haven't helped AT ALL.'

'Don't be glum, Penfold!' said Danger Mouse. 'We've still got to escape from

our ice prison, find Baron Greenback and outwit him in a series of fast-paced, daredevil adventures that'll have the readers on the edge of their seats until page 148. There'll be more than enough for you to do. I couldn't be the world's best secret agent without you.'

Oh, crikey. I really, really hoped he was right.

CHAPTER FOUR

'Take that!' yelled Danger Mouse. 'And that! And THAT!' His Mouse Fu high kicks bounced harmlessly off the icicles.

'Excuse me, Chief?' I said. 'Why don't you wait for me to finish cutting a Danger-Car-shaped hole with this ICEBLASTER?' Squawkencluck had converted it from the blowtorch I use to toast crème caramels. (Mmm . . . crème

caramels.) 'If you're patient for just another four hours, then we can simply fly out. Whoosh. See? Whoosh. Easy.'

'Heroes aren't patient, Penfold,' Danger Mouse told me seriously. 'Danger waits for no mouse. Take *that*, icicles!'

Outside, it was getting frostier and frostier. Claudia Day – London's leading weather forecaster – was on the big screen. 'It's cold!' she squeaked. 'And it's getting colder! The temperature is dropping faster than a barrel down a waterfall! It's chillier than Chile! As I speak, the ice caps are growing and creeping closer and closer, and when they meet it will be like LIVING IN THE ARCTIC.' She took a breath. 'Talking of

which, it might be a good idea to stock
up on a few emergency items for your
fridge-freezers . . . IN CASE OF ARCTIC
APOCALYPSE.'

Crikey. That was a good point. We
were down to our last fourteen litres of
milk. (Super secret agents drink a lot of
it.) I watched a crowd of panic buyers
stampede past HQ towards the local
supermarket as I pressed the turbo button
on the ice blaster. *Prrrrrrrrrp!* Just three
hours and fifty-eight minutes to freedom.

Or it would have been, if Professor
Squawkencluck hadn't arrived a few
moments later.

'Ah, Professor!' said Danger Mouse.
'Have you come to reveal your much more

brilliant invention that will allow us to escape from HQ in seconds rather than hours, foil Baron Greenback's wicked plans for world frostification and get back in time for tea?'

'No, I've brought these,' Professor Squawkencluck said proudly.

There was a pause.

'Well, I wasn't expecting those,' said Danger Mouse at last.

'Me neither,' I agreed. 'Although we should probably tell the readers what we're looking at, don't you think? Otherwise they might be imagining all sorts of brilliant inventions, like, say, rocket-powered ice skates or a kettle powered by nuclear fusion. Or something.'

Danger Mouse shrugged. 'Or you could just get the illustrator to draw them?'

'Top plan, Chief,' I said.

So here they are . . .

'This may seem a silly question, Professor,' Danger Mouse began, 'but how are two snowman suits going to help us save the world?'

'Aha.' Squawkencluck smiled knowingly. 'These were the obvious next step after my solar flares. There's no way these are going to rip. And when they're switched off they are simply warm and cosy snowman suits – furry on the outside and furry on the INSIDE – that will keep the wearer warm down to temperatures of -273°C. As I'm sure you know, -273°C is absolute zero. So it's not going to get any colder than that.'

'Yes, yes,' said Danger Mouse hurriedly. 'Absolutely, um, zero.'

'But,' Squawkencluck went on, 'when the suits are activated – by squeezing this realistic carrot nose – they make the wearers invisible, which is why I have named them . . . INVISIBLATORS.'

'Thanks, Professor!' said Danger Mouse. 'Come on, Penfold. I'll help you try yours on! Let's give it a test drive!'

Oh, crikey! Was that wise? I did rather like the idea of being invisible in the face of danger, but I also liked reading the instructions before trying out one of Squawkencluck's brand-new inventions. What if I vanished . . . and never reappeared?

Too late.

'*Pfoof*,' I said. There was no danger of

frostbite inside an invisiblator. I might be roasted or poached or fried or boiled or steamed or slow-cooked, but I definitely wouldn't be frozen. It was hotter than the centre of the sun in here.

'Let's try this baby out,' said Danger Mouse.

He tweaked my carrot nose.

'Invisible!' he said delightedly.

He tweaked it again.

'Visible!'

Tweak. *Invisible*. Tweak. Visible. Tweak. *Invisible*. Tweak. Visible. Tweak. *Invisible*. Tweak. Visible. Tweak. *Invisible*. Tweak. Visible. Tweak. *Invisible*. Tweak. Visible. Tweak. *Invisible*. Tweak. Visible. Tweak. *Invisible*. Tweak. Visible. Tweak.

Invisible. Tweak. Visible. Tweak. *Invisible*.
Tweak. Visible. Tweak. *Invisible*. Tweak.
Visible. Tweak. *Invisible*. Tweak. Visible.
Tweak. *Invisible*. Tweak. Visible. Tweak.
Invisible. Tweak. Visible. Tweak. *Invisible*.
Tweak. Visible –

'Stop!' I said, pulling off my snowman head and blinking sweat out of my eyes. I stared enviously at Danger Mouse, who looked as suave and laid-back as ever. Why couldn't I be that cool? 'We're not going to have enough room for the adventure in this book if you keep making me vanish and reappear. It wastes a lot of paper.'

ARGH! Suddenly we were blasted with sounds so loud and horrible they made my ears hurt. Honestly, it was SO BAD it made an unsupervised school orchestra sound brilliant.

Ding-a-ling! went a noise like the school bell for the end of break.

Parp! went a sound like a foghorn.

Pop-goes-the-weasel! tinkled what sounded like an ice-cream van.

But imagine all of those noises ALL AT THE SAME TIME.

'What's happening?' cried Danger Mouse. He leapt into a Mouse Fu crane pose. And then a monkey pose, a tiger pose, a viper pose, a mantis pose and a panda pose for good measure. 'Are we under attack?'

'Maybe it's an alert to tell us the end of the chapter is approaching!' I yelled over the noise.

'It's the alarm I set when I super-boosted the central-heating system earlier,' Squawkencluck said gleefully. 'It means that HQ is now officially defrosted and all entrances are clear. Look!'

Danger Mouse and I looked. Hurray! The icicles were gone. We were *free*!

'Come on, Penfold!' said Danger Mouse, shoving his snowman suit in the boot of the Mark IV, which was remarkably spacious for such a high-performance vehicle.

'Yes, Chief!' I cried. I wasn't going to lose confidence now. I was the world's

greatest super secret agent's sidekick –
and it was time to save the world.

Peowwwwwwwwww!

CHAPTER FIVE

Danger Mouse gripped the steering wheel as we skidded through the streets of London. 'Wheeeeeeeee!' he cried, flashing past frozen puddles. Lamp posts were hung with icicles that reached down towards the sparkling pavements. 'The road is so clear! The tarmac is so slippy! Do I have time to do a doughnut?'

'Nooooooo!' I yelled, hanging on to my snowman head. 'We're trying to stop an evil villain in just 148 pages. We're not spinning round in circles so that passers-by can cheer at silly tricks.'

'Ah, yes. Quite right,' Danger Mouse said. He stopped beside a newspaper noticeboard. 'Hello, what's going on *here*?'

WOOLLY-JUMPER SHORTAGE, the sign read. SHEEP FARMS RAIDED!

Oh, dear. Things were bad indeed.
Especially for the sheep.

Meanwhile, not so very far away,
Greenback was relaxing in his supersized
lunchbox in the Fiendish Fridge-freezer.

'How does the FFF work, *barone*?'
said Stiletto.

'Absolutely no idea,' said Baron
Greenback, with a shrug. 'I didn't get
to be an arch-villain by paying attention
in science at school. I let my minions do
that. Take Isambard King Kong Brunel,
for example. He invented the FFF so I
didn't have to. He's written a manual but
I am of course far too busy taking over
the world and generally wreaking havoc
to read it.'

'Ah, *si*,' said Stiletto. 'Silly me.'

Baron Greenback grinned evilly.
'All I know is that the more I turn the
thermostat to the right, the more I
deep-freeze the world,' he said. 'Cool,
huh? *Cooooool*. See, I'm hilarious!
Mwah ha ha!'

'H-h-h-hey!' shouted a snowman, as
Danger Mouse and I whizzed by.

Crikey. Were people that cold? Or had
Squawkencluck already mass-produced
her invisiblators in Swindon and sold
them on the internet in the time it took us
to get here?

'W-w-w-wait f-f-f-for m-m-m-me!' the
snowman pleaded.

'No can do!'
Danger Mouse
called back over his
shoulder. 'You're not
this book's bad guy,
I'm afraid. Sorry
about that!'

'G-g-g-grrrrrrr!'
the snowman
shivered, hurling a
carrot bullet after us.

'Who was that, Chief?' I asked as we
shot away, the carrot bouncing harmlessly
off the bulletproof – and, apparently,
carrot-proof – Mark IV.

'The Snowman,' replied Danger
Mouse. 'Villain. Can't stand the cold.

Loves barbecues. Melts a lot. He'll try to achieve world domination another week, don't worry.'

'Just trying to scare them, eh, *barone*?' Stiletto said to the Baron. 'If world leaders don't hand over one squillion pounds, you're not *really* going to deep-freeze everything? Are you *that* cold-hearted?'

'Yes,' said Baron Greenback. 'I am.'

'Oh, *barone* . . .' Stiletto smiled happily, holding his hands in the shape of a heart.

'DANGER MOUSE!' I shouted. 'Danger ahead! Slow down!'

'All under control, Penfold,' said Danger Mouse, sliding expertly to a halt behind a slow-moving queue of ice-cream vans. They were all playing Mozart's *Requiem*, which, apart from not being a particularly easy tune to dance to, wasn't going to encourage anyone to buy an ice cream. (In other words, it was A Bit Glum.) 'What's going on?' Danger Mouse called, reaching up to tap on the window of the last van.

'It's August,' the ice-cream seller replied miserably. 'It's the middle of summer. It's supposed to be sunny and it's supposed be my busiest month. But here I am with a freezer full of ice lollies and it's so cold that *no one* is stopping me and buying one. So I'm on strike. And so are all my mates. We're going to parade through the streets of London until someone takes notice.'

Oh, dear me. First, a woolly-jumper shortage. Now an ice-cream overload. It was an increasingly desperate situation. Sadly, I watched the queue of ice-cream vans shrink in the rear-view mirror as we sped away. But I wasn't sad just because I felt really sorry for them. If Danger Mouse had only stopped for long enough, I would have *loved* a ninety-nine.

'Um . . . *barone*?' said Stiletto.

'What now?' growled Baron Greenback. 'If I'd known you were going to ask this

many questions, I'd have hired a quiz master
to help me take over the world.'

Stiletto shivered inside his trench
coat. 'I'm cold, *barone*. How about you
pay me extra for working under extreme
conditions?'

'Put an extra coat on,' said Baron
Greenback. 'And button it.'

'Penfold, we're there!' said Danger Mouse,
slowing down a little.

'*There?*' I said. '*Here?* Are you *sure?*'
I looked up at the statue of Queen Victoria.
She had an unfortunate icicle hanging from
beneath her nose and didn't seem best
pleased to see us. 'Buckingham Palace?'

Danger Mouse nodded. He pulled a

lever and the Mark IV became briefly
airborne, shooting over the iron railings
and the heads of the shivering palace

guards, who were too frozen with surprise (and frost) to do anything. We touched down, rounded the palace and –

ZAP!

A flash of blue light hurtled towards us but with a breakneck swerve to the left Danger Mouse expertly dodged the deadly beam. A chilly-looking corgi dog wasn't so lucky. It was now trapped inside a block of corgi-shaped ice. I knew just how it felt.

'Aha!' said Danger Mouse. 'I see the Baron is using classic chill-ray technology. The question is, where *is* he?'

'Chief?' I said, my voice quivering. 'I think he might be inside *that*.'

The massive fridge-freezer loomed

above us, casting a dark shadow over
Buckingham Palace. It was tall, silver and
plastered with fridge magnets. Really BIG
ones. There were two doors – a large one
at the bottom, which must be the fridge,
and a smaller one, way, way above us.
I had a funny feeling that was the freezer,
and where we'd find the Baron. (Mostly
because that was where the chill rays were
coming from.)

Zap! Zap! Zappity-zap!

Danger Mouse dodged the deadly
beams with the skill of a long-time gamer.
He ducked and dived. He shimmied and
shook. But how long could he avoid them?

ZAP!

About that long.

The Mark IV lit up like the Las Vegas
skyline and came to a sudden halt.

Uh-oh. Was this really GAME OVER?

'Yes!' cried Baron Greenback, with a rock-star air-grab. 'I spy two snowmen outside! I have frozen Danger Mouse and his foolish sidekick SOLID. Now I shall become the controller of the universe!'

'I thought you were just going for world domination this time?' said Stiletto.

Baron Greenback was busy pulling something red, orange and yellow from behind the giant sandwich in the corner. 'Yeah, whatever. But there are 75 pages left, so I might as well take over a few bazillion galaxies too, just for the fun of it.' And he stepped into the multicoloured heap of fabric he'd just unearthed.

'So what are you doing *now*?' asked Stiletto.

The Baron rolled his eyes. 'I am quite clearly getting dressed up as an ice lolly,' he said. 'And before you ask any more questions . . . Firstly, it will stop me freezing once I climb out of this insulated lunchbox into the freezer compartment itself and, secondly, it will double as a handy disguise in case anyone spots my FFF and wonders why there's a handsome toad in the freezer compartment.'

'Oh,' said Stiletto, watching as Baron Greenback struggled into a rocket-shaped ice-lolly outfit. 'Right. So you've *definitely* defeated Danger Mouse?'

'If you don't believe me –' growled the Baron, stabbing at a button on his watch – 'then what's that?'

An image of the Mark IV pinged into life on the watch face. Beside it were two snowmen, shaped exactly like Danger Mouse and me.

'Danger Mouse is out of the way and my fiendish plan is working perfectly. It's now time to chill the world just a little bit more! Soon I'll have ONE SQUILLION POUNDS. And there's nothing anyone can do to stop me!'

Stiletto waited.

'Sorry,' said the Baron. 'I keep forgetting. Mwah ha ha!' Then he slowly pushed open the lunchbox lid and reached to turn the thermostat to the right.

'Wake up, Planet Earth!' he boomed. 'Time to freeze!'

CHAPTER SIX

'Is it safe to move yet, Chief?'
I whispered, peering up at the
freezer door.

See? There was no need to worry!
When the chill ray hit the Mark IV,
Danger Mouse cut all power and
activated the anti-frost shields. So all
the energy from the sub-zero beam was
converted back into heat and instead of
being frozen to death, it felt a bit like

sitting near a log fire. (A safe distance
from a log fire, obviously. Behind a
fireguard. You can never be too careful.)
Once we stopped, Danger Mouse got his
invisiblator suit out of the boot and high-
kicked his way inside it in seconds. Then
we stood motionless beside the Mark IV,
as warm as toast. (Mmm . . . toast.)

'Let's go, Penfold!' said Danger Mouse.
'The Baron thinks we're history, so he
won't be expecting us. All we have to
do is get inside the FFF and put him out
of action before he has a chance to turn
everything to ice. Come on. Chop-chop!'

I stared up at the towering kitchen
appliance – but not for too long because
the clouds floating high above made me

feel a bit dizzy – and spotted something
very useful. Stairs! Great. We would be
inside the FFF in no time. And I would
have shown what a brilliant sidekick I
could be, and Danger Mouse would be so
impressed that he'd never mind my danger-
phobia again. 'Look!' I whispered. 'St–'

'Shhh!' hissed Danger Mouse. 'I have a
brilliant plan!'

And, faster than you can eat a packet
of biscuits, I was wearing a bullet-shaped
helmet, a harness and a backpack . . .
sitting inside a slingshot . . . which
was suspended from a huge triangular
wooden frame . . . at the end of a long
wooden arm . . . balanced with a large
weight labelled: VERY HEAVY.

Oh. My. Giddy. Aunt. This. Was. So.
Terrifying. That. Suddenly. I. Could.
Not. Write. Sentences. Longer. Than.
One. Word.

'What do you think of my trebuchet?'
said Danger Mouse proudly, wheeling it
into position and vaulting on board.

'It's . . . erm . . . great,' I said. 'Where did
you find a catapult from the Middle Ages?'

'Under the spare wheel in the Mark IV,
of course,' he replied with a wink.

'But what about the st–' I squeaked.

'No time for chit-chat!' said the world's greatest secret agent. 'Three, two, one . . . Lift off! Wheeeeeeeeeeeee!'

We flew high into the air, up, up, up, until we were even higher than the FFF. Then we shot right over it and then – oh, no! – we were falling down, down, down the other side, and hurtling straight for one of the windows in a room on the top floor of Buckingham Palace. And this room was bound to be one of the Queen's special chambers, because that's the sort of thing that happens when you hang around with Danger Mouse. Trust me, it would never have been anything boring like the airing cupboard.

I shut my eyes and prepared for certain embarrassment.

But it was my lucky day – if you don't count the being-frozen-in-a-block-of-ice bit in Chapter One, obviously – and without warning we were yanked out of the catapult and floating back towards the FFF, hanging beneath two parachutes. (So that was what was in the backpacks.)

'Hold tight, Penfold,' warned Danger Mouse, grabbing my hand. 'This is the difficult part.'

Really? Oh, crikey. I was sort of hoping we'd done the difficult part already. I was looking forward to the part where we sat down with a nice cup of tea and a scone with jam and cream. (Mmm . . . jam and cream.)

Danger Mouse pulled a massive grappling hook out of his back pocket. He whirled it round until it became a blur, then hurled it in the direction of the FFF's roof. The metal hook dug in like a knife into soft butter. Pulling hand over hand on the rope, we were soon safe. OK, safe-ish. Let's face it, we were still on top of a skyscraper-sized fridge-freezer. It was never going to be my comfort zone.

'Having fun yet, Penfold?' asked Danger Mouse. 'Isn't this great! Isn't this dangerous! Now, all we've got to do is cut a trapdoor in the FFF roof using the miniature circular saw on my key ring and we'll be able to get on with defeating the Baron!'

'B-b-b-but . . .' I began. 'WHAT ABOUT THE ST–?'

Danger Mouse stopped, his circular saw already buzzing. 'I'm so sorry, Penfold. I'm so busy saving the world that I keep missing what you're trying to tell me. Come on, spit it out. What is this *st*–? Steak-and-kidney pie? Standing lamp? Starstruck fan with a spare helicopter?'

Yay! Danger Mouse was listening to

me! And I'd discovered something truly
astonishing that would help us to beat Baron
Greenback together. This time, I wasn't
going to be the one trying to keep up. Danger
Mouse was going to be so proud of me.

'*Stairs*, Chief,' I said proudly. 'There's a
spiral staircase running up one side of the
FFF. We could have climbed up it to reach
Baron Greenback's lair, but it'll still be
useful now. Look, there's the top of it over
there. If we climb down a little way, we can
open up the door into the freezer and just
step inside.' I beamed so wide, one cheek
was in Ealing and the other in West Ham.

'*Bor-ing!*' sang Danger Mouse.

My heart sank. It wasn't boring. (OK,
maybe a *little* bit.)

'Look here, Penfold,' said Danger Mouse. 'My name's not Safety Mouse. If we're going to foil the Baron's wicked plan, we're going to do it the DANGEROUS way. But first, let's get invisible!' He grabbed my carrot nose and gave it a firm tweak, then did the same to his own – and just like that . . . *we were gone.*

(Except we weren't. We were still standing on the roof of the FFF. But you know what I mean.)

Bzzzt! Danger Mouse plunged the whirring blade into the roof, cut a circular hole round himself and jumped hard on the metal beneath his feet. With a creak and a crack and a SNAP, the metal trapdoor and Danger Mouse plunged into the freezing depths.

'Danger Mouse . . . ?' I whispered down the hole. What did I do now? Jump into oblivion? Er, no. I would follow the appropriate health-and-safety regulation and go via the stairs with the handrail, making sure to hold tight. And if I could get hold of a hard hat from somewhere, then I would wear one of those too.

Or rather, I would have done, if Danger Mouse hadn't reached an arm back out of the hole, grabbed me and yanked me in after him. I tumbled into the freezing depths head first, landing in a heap beside him . . . *just* as the lid of a seriously big lunchbox lifted to reveal PROBABLY THE SCARIEST THING EVER.

'Whoa,' said Danger Mouse.

'Crikey,' I added.

'Are you going to tell our Danger Fans what just climbed out of the world's biggest lunchbox and is lumbering towards us right now?' whispered Danger Mouse.

'Not yet, Chief,' I whispered back. 'Because if I keep its identity a secret

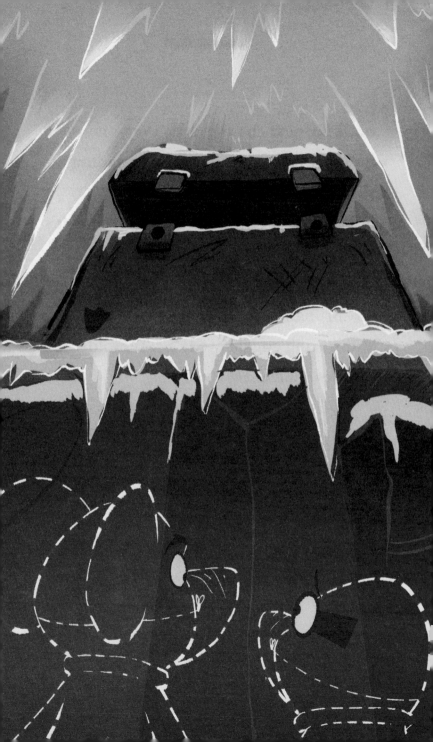

until the next chapter, then everyone will
be super curious and will keep reading
to find out what PROBABLY THE
SCARIEST THING EVER actually is. It's
called suspense, apparently. All the best
authors do it.'

'Brilliant,' whispered Danger Mouse,
still staring goggle-eyed. 'Er, Penfold?'

'Yes, Chief?'

'Do you think it might be a good time
to start Chapter Seven now? Only it's
getting really, really close . . .'

CHAPTER SEVEN

I t was big.

It was rocket-shaped.

It was red, orange and yellow.

And it was heading straight for us.

'Quick, Penfold!' whispered Danger
Mouse. 'Over here!'

He beckoned urgently from behind
a box of fish fingers the size of a double
wardrobe and I scooted over to join him,
just as the biggest rocket-shaped ice lolly

I'd ever seen thundered past our hiding place and headed towards a half-empty packet of frozen peas. (I think they were frozen peas. The few that had spilled out were so totally huuuuuge, they might just as easily have been exercise balls.)

'Well, you don't see that every day,' whispered Danger Mouse.

I nodded, even though I was invisible. You didn't see massively magnified freezer compartments every day either, stuffed with trifles the size of bouncy castles (stamped with **BEST BEFORE: LAST CENTURY**). Or pizzas as big as ice rinks. Or plastic containers the size of pick-up trucks filled with frozen brown slop. Or frozen oven chips as big as planks of wood, for that matter.

'Why is everything so *big*, DM?' I muttered. It was very odd speaking to someone that I couldn't see.

'Hmm . . .' said Danger Mouse. 'I expect it was magnified at the same time that the real fridge-freezer was supersized.'

'And why didn't they pick something a bit more, well, small to take over the world in?' I asked. 'I'm sure Greenback could've got an evil scientist to supercharge the motor of a normal fridge-freezer and had the same effect.'

'True,' said Danger Mouse's voice. 'But if there's one thing I've learned during my long-running and highly successful career of saving the planet and occasionally the universe, in which I've used my incredible skills and many, many talents to fight evil . . . it's that bad guys just can't help showing off.'

'Oh,' I said. 'Right.' And it looked as if he was right, because the world's most

terrifying frozen-fruit-juice-based dessert
started to speak . . .

'I'm the GREATEST,' he shouted.
'I'm FANTASTIC.'

He was stealing Danger Mouse's lines!
Who would dare to do such a thing?

Had our hero finally met his match?
Was this a new terrifying ice-lolly villain?

'Victory is within my grasp!' roared
the giant ice lolly. 'I am about to achieve
world frostification! And where is
everyone's hero, the great Danger Mouse?
He's frozen solid on the doorstep with
that idiot sidekick of his. He wasn't even
clever enough to find his way inside the
FFF. Mwah ha ha!'

'Baron Greenback!' I gasped.

There was no reply.

'Chief?' I whispered. 'Are you still there?'

'I'm just rolling my eyes, Penfold,' replied Danger Mouse. 'Try to keep up. I worked out that it was Baron Greenback two pages ago. It's not a particularly good disguise and, anyway, can you think of any other master criminals who are likely to be stomping about in Fiendish Fridge-freezers in London this week?'

'Good point,' I said. My heart sank. Baron Greenback thought I was an idiot. And now I'd let Danger Mouse down. Again. What if he traded me in for a far cleverer, more exciting sidekick who wasn't such a party pooper when it came to health and safety? Now that I'd had that thought, I couldn't get rid of it again. Oh, CRUMBS. And talking of crumbs, there were fish-finger crumbs everywhere. Fish-finger manufacturers really do need to think of a way to glue them on better.

All this time, the freezer had been whirring noisily in the background, like a biplane struggling to take off.

'Sooooooo much electricity!' the Baron cried gleefully. 'Oodles and oodles of kilowatts! Just think of the electricity bill at Buckingham Palace next quarter! Mwah ha ha! It'll be a Right Royal Bill!'

Ha! Actually, that was quite funny. Though I suspected the Queen might not agree.

'Caw!' someone cawed. It was Stiletto, the world's

meanest crow. He looked chilly in his thin, flappy trench coat and it reminded me that we were in a freezer. It was quite easy to forget when you were snuggled inside a warm, toasty invisiblator.

'Ah, there you are,' Baron Greenback said to Stiletto. 'Have you come to tell me that seventeen world leaders have emailed to say they're giving me ONE SQUILLION POUNDS and are asking if I would like it in fifties or hundreds?'

'Er . . . no,' said Stiletto. 'No one's emailed. Except for Isambard King Kong Brunel, who says you haven't paid him for the FFF yet.'

'*Rarrrrrr!*' roared the Baron. 'How did that sound?' he asked Stiletto. 'Only

I thought I might have a change from the mwah-ha-has.'

'Stick with the evil laughter, *barone*,' said the crow. 'More evil genius, less London Zoo.'

'Fair enough,' said Baron Greenback. 'Just thought I'd ask. Right, where was I? Ah, yes. TIME TO TURN DOWN THE HEAT.'

'Shouldn't that be "turn up the cold", *barone*?' asked his right-hand crow.

'Whatever!' snapped the Baron. 'I've printed myself out a licence to chill and I'm going to use it. And soon this planet's foolish inhabitants will be sooooo coooold they'll do anything I say. MWAH HA HA!'

His manic laugh echoed nastily off the enormous lumpy purple bag on the top shelf filled with last summer's forgotten fruit. I couldn't help thinking that it would be perfect for a crumble. (Probably about forty-two crumbles, actually.)

'I don't think we're going to hear anything useful hiding away back here. He's just blowing his own horn, and nobody likes that!' hissed Danger Mouse. 'Time for action! *Ready?*'

'I'm ready, Chief!' I replied.

'*Steady?*' said Danger Mouse, unzipping his invisiblator and pulling out Squawkencluck's super-cool hairdryer. He pointed to a brand-new red button labelled: DEFROST-FROZEN-EVIL-LAIRS-TO-STOP-VILLAINS-TAKING-OVER-THE-WORLD SETTING.

DEFROST-
FROZEN-EVIL-LAIRS-
TO-STOP-VILLAINS-
TAKING-OVER-
THE-WORLD
SETTING

Brilliant.

'Steady, Chief!' I whispered, as Danger Mouse zipped up his invisiblator again so all that could be seen of the world's greatest super secret agent was a floating hairdryer.

'*Go!*' hissed Danger Mouse.

But, just before Danger Mouse could start zapping, something bad happened.

Actually, no. Something TRULY
AWFUL. (I can hardly bear to write it
down. But if I don't it'll make no sense
when I shout 'Nooooooo!' on the next
page. So here goes, Danger Fans . . .)

Not only was the snowman suit furry
on the outside, it was furry on the inside
too. And it was tickling my nose.

'Aaaah . . .' I said. 'Aaaah . . .
AAATISHOOO!'

It was the biggest sneeze in the history
of sneezes.

BUT THAT'S NOT THE WORST BIT.

When I sneezed, I grabbed my nose –
not my actual nose, but my carrot nose.
And when I grabbed my carrot nose I
became one hundred per cent visible.

AND THAT'S STILL NOT THE WORST BIT.

When I grabbed my nose, I whacked Danger Mouse's nose with my elbow, which meant that he became visible too!

Now we were both visible. (OK, you can relax now. THAT ACTUALLY WAS THE WORST BIT.)

'Nooooooo!' I shouted.

CHAPTER EIGHT

'Freeze!' yelled Baron Greenback. Which, seeing as the FFF and the whole of London were freezing already, was a bit unnecessary.

Danger Mouse shook his head. 'I'm afraid I won't be doing that, Greenback. Nobody is freezing today!'

'We'll see about that,' said the Baron. 'I've got this far, Danger Mouse. You can't stop me now.' He paused and frowned. 'Unless you want to give me one squillion pounds, that is. *Then* I'll stop.'

'Nice try, Baron,' said Danger Mouse. 'But, as Penfold puts all my cash into a high-interest savings account with ninety days' notice for withdrawals, I couldn't give you any money even if I wanted to. Which, of course, I don't.'

'Then you leave me with no choice,' said Greenback. 'I'm going to turn the thermostat to REALLY QUITE COLD NOW and watch your beloved England freeze.' He raced towards the big round knob on the other side of the freezer.

Quick as a flash, Danger Mouse whizzed straight after him.

Boing! He bounced off the sherry

trifle box. *Boing!* He hit the fish fingers.
Thud thud thud thud thud! He ran along
the side of the FFF. *Dink dink dink!* He
sprinted along the ice-cube tray and leapt
into frosty nothingness.

'Since when did you learn free
running?' I gasped, chasing after him at
floor level.

Danger Mouse paused in mid-air and
smoothed his eyebrow. 'Cool, huh?' he said.
'I watched it on the telly last week. I figured
it would be easy for someone as super sporty

as me. And what do you know . . . it is!'

'Wow,' I sighed, in awe.

'Actually,' said Danger Mouse, who was still in mid-air, 'this illustration would look great on the back of the toilet door in HQ.

Do you think the illustrator could sketch me one at A3 size? Great. Right. Back to the nail-biting adventure!'

He dropped, landed neatly on all fours, then sprang up and ran after the Baron, who was finding it difficult to run in his ice-lolly outfit and waddled along like a bear carrying too much shopping.

By now, Danger Mouse was hot on his heels. But the Baron was one step ahead – if anyone's interested, I was about seventeen steps behind – and he hurled himself at the thermostat and hung on tight.

'*Oh, no you don't!*' shouted Danger Mouse.

'*Oh, yes he does!*' I joined in. Oooh, this was fun.

Both the rocket ice-lolly and the
snowman swung round and glared at me.

'Oops. Sorry.' I smiled apologetically.
'So this *isn't* the bit where we do a panto?'

'No,' said Danger Mouse. 'It isn't. Do
keep up, Penfold.'

'OK, Chief,' I said, shifting from
one snowman foot to another. The
invisiblator suit was now so warm that
it was a bit like walking on hot coals.
'Although I should probably mention that
HE'S BEHIND YOU.'

'Really, Penfold?' Danger Mouse
flipped back his snowman head and
raised an eyebrow. 'And I suppose he's
wielding an ice-lolly stick and getting
ready to bop me on the head with it?'

'Er . . . yes,' I said. *How did he know?*
Danger Mouse grinned. 'Then that
proves Squawkencluck's all-new eyes-
in-the-back-of-my-head feature of the
EyePatch really does work.' He reached
out and plucked another ice-lolly stick
from a packet of real rocket ice lollies.

'Time for some ice hockey, Baron!' he shouted – and whacked a stray supersized pea straight at him.

The Baron whacked it back.

Danger Mouse walloped it high.

The Baron hooked it out of mid-air and clouted it right at Danger Mouse's carrot nose, which wasn't a great idea because – *bonk!* – he disappeared. But the ice-lolly hockey stick didn't. I watched as the lump of wood floated eerily upward and twirled round before firing the pea towards the enormous frozen potato waffle at the far end of the FFF.

'Goal!' Danger Mouse cried, reappearing with a carroty tweak. 'I win!'

'Oh, I don't *think* so,' said Baron

Greenback. And he turned the thermostat dial to HORRIBLY COLD.

'Yoo-hoo!'

Blimey. Could this freezer get any weirder? Because that voice sounded like it came from Outer Space . . .

'Up here, Penfold!'

Oh, no. Actually, it came from the top of a frosty box of Yorkshire puddings. (Mmm . . . Yorkshire puddings.)

'Danger Mouse?' I said. 'Is that you?'

'Of course it's me!' said Danger Mouse. 'Who did you think it was? An alien? Ha ha!'

'Hilarious,' said Baron Greenback. He stood in the middle of a puddle of frozen sticky stuff, wielding the world's

biggest Arctic roll. 'Excuse me, but has everyone forgotten I'm here? Does no one care that I'm FREEZING THE WORLD?'

'Of course we care, Baron,' said Danger Mouse. '*Geronimo!!!*'

Brilliant. Danger Mouse was now wearing lolly-stick skis! He pushed himself off the Yorkshire-pudding box, whizzed down the side of the frozen pizza leaning against it, hit an upturned Christmas pudding (**BEST BEFORE: 1972**) and – *whoosh!* – somersaulted like a Catherine wheel towards the Baron, knocking the Arctic roll right out of his hands with a perfectly timed Mouse Fu kick.

Kerpow!

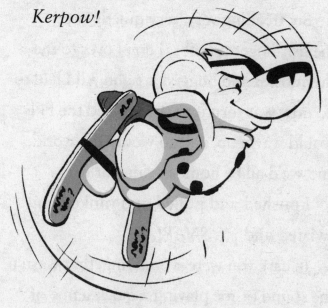

It was right then that I realized no one was watching the thermostat — not even Stiletto, who was sneaking a scoop of ice cream out of a giant tub. This was my chance. I could totally save the world and Danger Mouse would never be disappointed in me again!

So, treading very, very quietly over the fish-finger crumbs, I crept over to the thermostat and hugged it tight. All I had to do now was turn it to the left and the FFF would warm up, and so would the world, and we'd all be home in time for tea.

I pushed and pulled and yanked and twisted and . . . *SNAP!*

In case you were wondering, that wasn't the sound of me playing a quick game of cards. That was the thermostat breaking.

And now it was pointing to ABSOLUTE ZERO.

CHAPTER NINE

PLANET EARTH AND EVERYONE ON IT WERE HEADING FOR DEEP FREEZE. And it was *all my fault*.

'Danger Mouse . . . ?' I said. I felt terrible. I'd tried to help, but I'd just made things a squillion times worse.

'I'm terribly sorry, Penfold,' replied Danger Mouse, aiming a karate kick at the Baron, who ducked and retaliated with a left hook. 'I'm a bit busy right

now, saving the world. Can it wait?'

'Erm . . . not really.' I edged closer to the fight.

'Ooh, look, Danger Mouse!' The Baron laughed, dodging punches. 'Here's your sidekick. He probably needs saving again.'

My jaw dropped. How did he *know*?

'Ah, not Penfold,' said Danger Mouse proudly. 'He can look after himself – and me. Did I ever tell you about the time that he singlehandedly tasted all the tea in China to make sure that I'd have the very best cuppa?'

I gulped. Had Danger Mouse bumped his head? I knew for a fact that he'd rescued me at least twenty-seven times. And that was only last week. Unless he was just . . . standing up for me? Oh, dear. That only made me feel worse. I'd let him down so badly.

Baron Greenback laughed nastily. 'Let me know when your sidekick's done something *really* worthwhile, Danger Mouse,' he said. 'Like learning to ride a bike without stabilizers! Ha ha –'

Danger Mouse hurled a snowball at him.

'Now, Penfold,' he said, throwing an arm round my shoulders. 'What was it you wanted to talk to me about?'

I gulped. 'Er . . . nothing much, Chief,' I said. 'Nothing I can't handle on my own, that is.'

Danger Mouse nodded. 'Cool. Well, if you don't mind, I've sort of got to defeat this evil supervillain right now. So I'll catch you later?'

'Great,' I said. 'See ya!'

Because suddenly I had a plan. I know! Get me! And it was a completely ace plan too, one that Danger Mouse himself would be proud of. I took a deep breath. I could do this.

Dodging past Stiletto, who was still

slurping ice cream and looking a bit green now, I ran for the exit. The *real* exit. The one at the top of the spiral staircase that I'd spotted earlier. This time I was in charge and I wasn't going to do anything dangerous like slide from the top of the FFF on a zip wire or dive into oblivion on a gigantic paper plate.

I was going to walk down the stairs.

And I was going to hold on to the handrail to make sure I didn't slip.

Because that's how I roll.

Five hundred and seventy-two stairs later, I was back down to earth – slippery, icy, frozen earth – with my genius plan to defrost it. I was going to pull the plug on

Baron von Greenback's evil plans.

No, really. I was actually going to pull out the plug.

Think back, Danger Fans . . .

Remember earlier, when Baron Greenback was boasting about the size of the royal electricity bill next quarter? Well, that made me think. If HRH was going to have a massive electricity bill, then THE FFF MUST BE PLUGGED IN AT BUCKINGHAM PALACE. So all I had to do was follow the electricity cable to the socket and pull out the plug. Once the power was cut, the FFF would stop freezing everything and – *ta-daaaaa!* – the world would defrost.

Simple.

I scurried round the back of the FFF
and looked for the power lead. There it
was: a big, black winding snake of a thing,
wiggling towards the royal palace. Ooh,
this was GREAT. So exciting! I might ask
Danger Mouse if I could be in charge more
often! Perhaps every second Thursday.

Wheeeeeeeeeee!

(Ahem. Excuse me, lovely illustrator.
Any chance you could capture the moment?
You can? Excellent. And you'll make me
look really cool? Just this once? Yay!)

In my very best surf pose I skidded
right across the icy square behind
Buckingham Palace. Then I stopped at
the back door. Or, to be more accurate, I
crashed into the back door at top speed,

came to a shuddering halt, bashed my
carrot nose, vanished, tweaked my nose
and reappeared.

I tapped politely. 'Anyone at home?'

There was no reply.

Nervously, I pushed open the door.
Wow. Amazing. I wished Danger Mouse
was there to see this. There were green
welly boots EVERYWHERE. Shelf
upon shelf of wellies. Entire walls of
the rubbery things. Hundreds of them.
How many feet did HRH have? Was she
a mutant millipede in disguise? I made
a note, just in case Planet Earth was
attacked by one next week and we were
looking for suspects.

By the time it reached Buckingham

Palace, the FFF's massive cable had
shrunk, almost as if Isambard King Kong
Brunel's technical wizardry only worked
over a certain distance. (Or perhaps
Brunel couldn't be bothered to supersize
the socket too.) I followed it into the
welly-boot room until it became lost in a
tangle of cables and several multi-socket
extension leads.

My hand hovered over the plugs.
Which one should I pull out? Which one
would cut the power to the FFF and stop
the deadly deep freeze?

CHAPTER TEN

Desperate situations didn't get much more desperate than this.

Danger Mouse was battling Baron Greenback in the Fiendish (and now very, very Frosty) Fridge-freezer. But unless he'd brought a screwdriver with him, he wasn't going to be able to fix the thermostat.

Meanwhile, I was staring at four identical plugs, trying to work out which belonged to the FFF. If I pulled out the right plug, I would save the world. But how did I know which plug was the right plug?

The answer was simple. I *didn't* know. So I took a deep breath and switched off the power at the wall.

Click!

Upstairs in the Queen's bedroom, the royal hairdryer stopped working. 'Lawks!' cried HRH to her lady-in-waiting. 'One looks as if one has been

electrocuted. Hmm. One quite likes it. Plenty of royal hairspray, please!'

In the royal control centre, the CCTV screens fizzled out. But, seeing as none

of the special forces seemed to have noticed that there was a fridge-freezer the size of Big

Ben in the backyard, this didn't make an awful lot of difference to national security.

In the royal kitchen, the molten chocolate in the royal chocolate fountain – which was saved for very special occasions and under no circumstances should be plugged in on a Friday afternoon just so the staff could have a party – stopped cascading. So the kitchen staff shrugged and dipped ladles into the chocolate pool at the bottom instead. (Mmm . . . chocolate.)

And at the very same time, the FFF's massive motor whirred to a halt with a clattery *clunk* . . . and fell silent at last.

I cheered. High above, the FFF's freezer door whacked open as if had been karate chopped, which it probably had. Danger Mouse stood in the doorway, silhouetted against the freezer's light. Behind him, I could see Baron Greenback trapped in a prison made from giant frozen potato waffles.

'Bravo!' he cried.

'Yayyyyy!' I cheered, again. 'Well done, Chief!'

'Yes, I did do rather well, didn't I?' said Danger Mouse, parachuting down and landing on one toe before spinning slowly in front of the camera crews that had now appeared. 'But enough of this chit-chat. Cue the fireworks!'

Oh. I quietly rolled up the two-thousand-word thank-you speech I'd hastily written. It didn't look as if I was going to need it.

The celebrations were unbelievable – probably the third-best London had ever seen. Red, white and blue fireworks lit the sky and were reflected beautifully in the Thames. The Queen's sword was polished and ready to knight Danger Mouse. A World War One biplane took off, with a special banner on board. And, best of all, a new series of the *Danger Mouse* TV show was announced.

There was just one TINY problem.

The world was taking quite a while to defrost. Defrosting always does take *ages*, doesn't it? Even when you press the defrost button on the microwave – and, because Brunel hadn't bothered inventing a giant microwave, we didn't have that option.

'Cut the fireworks!' sighed the Prime Minister. 'Pop the Queen's sword on ice. And put the new series on hold!'

'Chief,' I said, climbing back inside the FFF, where Danger Mouse was throwing a frozen pea against the wall over and over again. I puffed out a plume of frosty air. 'Will the world defrost soon?'

'I suppose there's only one thing for it,' said Danger Mouse. 'Patience.'

It seemed an odd time for it, but hey ho. I pulled out a pack of playing cards and began dealing them.

'Good idea, Penfold,' said Danger Mouse. 'The world will defrost soon, don't worry. Any time, um . . . Well, actually, I've no idea. But soon. Probably. We should just wait and, erm, learn a new skill or something.'

'Or we could miss out the bit where I learn to crochet and you become fluent in Japanese and just finish the chapter here?' I suggested.

'Penfold, what a GREAT idea,' said Danger Mouse. 'What are we waiting for? Hurry up! Turn the page! Bring it on, Chapter Eleven!'

CHAPTER ELEVEN

*D*rip ... *Drip* ... *Drip* ... *Drop* ... *Drip* ... *Drippitty drip drop* ...

You get the idea.

Baron Greenback's deep freeze was over. The world was defrosting!

'ACTION!' said the Prime Minister.

Fireworks exploded, again!

The crowds cheered, again!

The new series went into pre-production, again!

DANGER MOUSE

And the World War One biplane that had been slowly circling since the middle of Chapter Ten finally unfurled its banner and pulled it across the skies of London. DANGER MOUSE DID IT AGAIN! the banner read.

'Good show, chaps!' said Colonel K, whose hologram was clad in a one-piece ski outfit and a woolly hat.

We were still in the FFF, keeping an eye on Baron Greenback. He glared angrily at us from the DIY prison Danger Mouse had built out of potato waffles. Behind him, Stiletto was curled up in an ice-cream tub, clutching his stomach.

'Er . . . What exactly did happen?' asked the Colonel. 'Only I was heavily involved in a very important case when all this kicked off and I sort of missed it.'

Squawkencluck, who'd caught the bus to Buckingham Palace to inspect the FFF, rolled her eyes and muttered, 'That means he fell asleep.'

'Oh, it was just another normal
Friday afternoon in the life of a top-
class super secret agent, sir,' said Danger
Mouse, leaning back against a box
of antique lasagne. 'Isn't that right,
Penfold?' he added.

I nodded sadly. This was it. Danger
Mouse was going to tell Colonel K that
I was too boring and sensible to be a
sidekick and he'd like to trade me in for
someone with a bit more pizazz. And
then there would be a national sidekick
competition, featured on successive
Saturday nights, in which the public
would vote for a replacement, and I
would have to learn how to dance the
quickstep in front of an audience of

millions to prove that I really was exciting
and daring BUT I WOULD LOSE.

'Marvellous,' said Colonel K. 'Well
done, Danger Mouse!'

'Actually, sir,' said Danger Mouse.
'I think you ought to be congratulating
Penfold.'

'What what?' said the Colonel.
'Penfold? Who the Dickens is that?'

'My brilliant sidekick, of course,' said
Danger Mouse, wearing a film-star grin.
'I might have saved the world, again, but
I couldn't have done it without dear old
Penfold.'

So Danger Mouse *had* been paying
attention! I was the second-greatest! I was
the second-most fantastic! Wherever there

was danger I'd be there too! I blushed so
much that I managed to defrost an entire
pepperoni pizza.

An ominous squelching noise from the back of the FFF stopped me before I could cook the pizza as well.

'Mwah ha ha!' cried the Baron, whose potato-waffle prison had now defrosted and sagged, allowing him to escape. Shedding his ice-lolly outfit, he dived into the only tub of ice cream that Stiletto hadn't eaten.

Brrrrrrrr! He rose slowly out of the cookies 'n' cream . . . riding Squawkencluck's airship!

'How's he doing that?' I whispered. 'I thought it was remote controlled.'

'It is,' Squawkencluck chipped in. 'But it can be operated manually too. Didn't I say?'

Ah. That might have been handy to know when I was bouncing around HQ in Chapter One.

'You've beaten me this time!' cried Baron Greenback. 'But I'll be back!'

He buzzed slowly away in the direction of west London.

We all waved goodbye.

'So have you got the remote control, Chief?' I asked.

'Oh, yes,' said Danger Mouse. 'But I'll give him a head start before I use it. I imagine they'd like to see the Baron perform a few loop-the-loops over Willesden Green.'

And we laughed all the way back to HQ.

So that's it for this time, folks. It turns out that being practical isn't such a bad thing after all. But I've decided that it might be a good idea to take time out from being sensible every now and again, which is why I've decided to finish this book with a picture of me taken when I was hang-gliding across the Grand Canyon, just this week. Don't I look **GREAT**?

Yours extremely dangerously,

Penfold

ACTIVITIES

1. Count Duckula got hold of this book during production. You know how much Duckula wants to be famous – he was desperate to get into the book somehow! See if you can spot every duck footprint he's managed to sneak on to the pages. There are 23 in total!

2. Penfold's favourite colour is top secret. (Not even Danger Mouse knows what it is. He thinks it's navy blue, but he's wrong.) Now YOU can discover the astonishing truth! Simply follow these clues to spell out the answer.
    - What is the first letter on page 104?
    - What is the third letter on page 74?
    - What is the seventh letter on page 53?
    - What is the twenty-first letter on page 35?
    - What is the thirty-fifth letter on page 42?

3. Follow the trails through the FFF's freezer compartment to locate Penfold's airship!

DANGER MOUSE

Also available

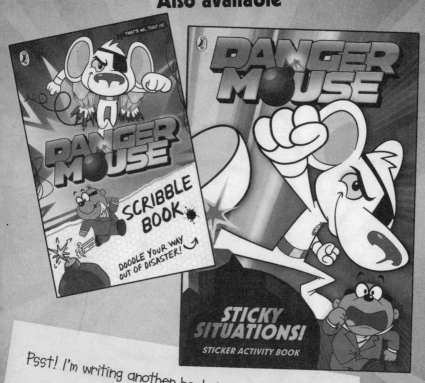

SCRIBBLE BOOK

DOODLE YOUR WAY OUT OF DISASTER!

STICKY SITUATIONS!

STICKER ACTIVITY BOOK